London's Burning

Stories linking with the History
National Curriculum.

To Trisha Mantle, a rising star.

First published in 1997 by Franklin Watts
96 Leonard Street, London EC2A 4XD

Franklin Watts Australia
56 O'Riordan Street, Alexandria, Sydney, NSW 2015

This edition published 2002
Text © Karen Wallace 1997

Editor: Matthew Parselle
Series Editor: Paula Borton
Designer: Kirstie Billingham
Consultant: Dr Anne Millard, BA Hons, Dip Ed, PhD

A CIP catalogue record for this book
is available from the British Library.

ISBN 0 7496 4595 4 (pbk)

Dewey Classification 942.06

Printed in Great Britain

London's Burning

by
Karen Wallace

Illustrations by Jamie Smith

FRANKLIN WATTS
LONDON•SYDNEY

A map of London, showing Pudding Lane

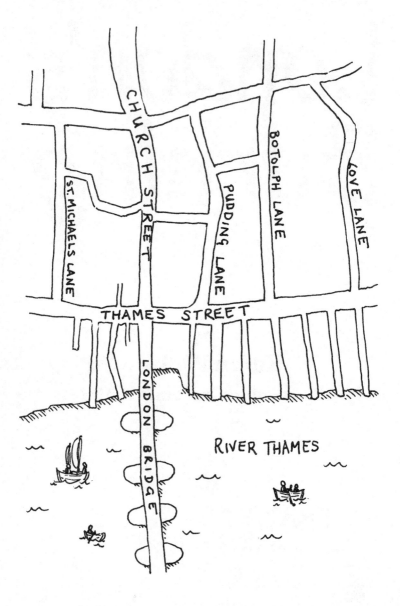

1

The King's Biscuits

Harriet Farynor stood in front of a long wooden table in her father's bakery in Pudding Lane. She dipped her hands in a pile of flour and picked up a lump of biscuit dough.

Behind her a dog barked.

At the other end of the kitchen, a huge joint of pork turned on a spit over a low red fire. The spit was attached to a large wooden wheel. Inside the wheel a terrier called Ginger was walking round and round and round. He barked again.

Harriet smiled and broke off a tiny bit of the dough. She walked over to Ginger and fed him the dough through the crisscross slats that kept him inside the wheel.

"What do you think you're doing, girl?" muttered a gruff voice behind her. "That dough's for the King's biscuits, not for your flea-bitten dog."

"It was just a tiny piece, Father," replied Harriet, quickly. She could feel her face going hot and red. "Besides, my flea-bitten dog is working hard cooking *your* food."

Thomas Farynor shrugged. He was a kind man and he knew how fond his daughter had become of the terrier since her mother had died of plague barely a year before.

He sniffed at a tiny iron door built into the brick wall. "Loaves are cooked," he said.

Inside the wall was a bee-hive shaped oven. Inside that were rows of round loaves, each one golden brown and stamped with Thomas Farynor's mark.

Harriet broke off a piece of the biscuit dough and rolled it into a rope. Then she took a length and twisted it into a curling knot.

Making these knot-shaped biscuits had been her mother's job. Harriet remembered watching her mother's small rough hands twisting and weaving the dough exactly as she was doing now.

She felt her father pat her on the shoulder. "You're a good girl," he said. "Your mother would be proud of you."

Harriet looked down at her knots. No two were the same. That was what King Charles II

had liked about them which was why he had placed a special order every week.

Thomas Farynor absent-mindedly broke off a piece of dough and put it into his mouth. There was a strong taste of caraway seed and a hint of their secret ingredient. The butter was washed with rosewater before it was mixed with the eggs, flour and other ingredients.

"Father!" said Harriet in a pretend reproving voice. "This dough's for the King's biscuits not for your afternoon snack."

"So it is," replied Thomas Farynor with a smile. "I'll taste them when they're baked." Then, as he had done a thousand times before, he opened the oven door with an iron bar and picked up a long-handled wooden paddle.

Harriet breathed in the delicious smell of newly baked bread as her father slid the paddle underneath the round loaves and lifted them carefully onto a cooling shelf on the other side of the room.

When all the loaves were out, he pushed the scattered embers into a neat pile on one side of the oven. At the same moment, Harriet arranged the last of the knot biscuits on a baking tray and held it out. Her father slid the paddle under the tray and put it into the oven.

As he shut the iron door, Harriet took a deep breath. It was the moment she had been waiting for all day. "May I take the King's biscuits to the Palace, Father," she asked.

Her father only grunted.

"You promised I might," said Harriet, hurriedly. Her stomach filled with butterflies. Thomas Farynor turned. His face was red and sweaty from the heat of the oven. "So I did, lass," he said. "And so you shall. Nelly will go with you. Her mother has a parcel to be taken to the Palace."

Harriet's pale round face broke into a grin. Nelly was her best friend and she lived at the end of Pudding Lane. Her mother was a lacemaker and made collars for the King. Sometimes Nelly was allowed to deliver them.

It would be a real adventure to go to the Palace at Whitehall together!

"And may I take Ginger?" asked Harriet. "He hasn't had a walk these past three days."

Thomas Farynor turned and looked at the huge joint of pork on the spit. It was obviously still far from cooked. "Ginger must finish his work," he replied in such a voice that Harriet didn't argue.

She wiped her floury hands on her apron. "I'll fetch the kindling for the next bake," she murmured.

"I'll send Walter," replied her father.

Walter was the odd jobs boy. He hadn't worked with them long and it looked as if he wouldn't be working with them for much longer either.

Walter was lazy and couldn't be trusted to do a job properly.

"Be sure to call in at Mistress Threadneedle's house," added her father as he turned and dragged a sack of flour from the store cupboard. "She's keeping a parcel for you, too."

Harriet stared at her father's broad back bent over the flour. What on earth was he talking about?

What sort of parcel could Nelly's mother be keeping for her?

Suddenly a wonderful idea exploded in Harriet's mind. Nelly's mother sometimes made skirts and dresses for her friends and family. Harriet hadn't worn new clothes for as long as she could remember.

"Father!" she cried, her eyes sparkling. "Is it something for me?"

"You'll find out," muttered Thomas Farynor from inside the store cupboard.

"Now get on with you, girl. The King's biscuits will be baked soon."

He turned to find the kitchen was empty. Harriet was already halfway down Pudding Lane, her feet barely touching the ground.

2

Fine Boating Weather

Later that day Nelly and Harriet set off
through the narrow streets, each with her
own parcel to take to the King. It was a
bright blue September afternoon and the
sun was warm on their hair.

Harriet couldn't remember feeling as

happy as this for years and years.

Nelly Threadneedle patted her friend's hand. "You look lovely in your new dress, Harriet," she said. "It's almost the same green as your eyes."

"Fit to visit a king, do you think?" asked Harriet with a grin. "I think that's why father gave it to me."

"Most certainly fit for a king," replied Nelly. "And with bringing him his favourite biscuits, I shouldn't be surprised if he gave you land and titles besides."

The two girls laughed and turned down towards the river. Great warehouses loomed on either side of them and the air was sharp with the smell of tallow, rope, oil and spices.

Alongside the river, timber and coal lay in huge piles on the wooden wharves. Everywhere men rushed about carrying hessian sacks or rolling great barrels of wine and brandy. All the while hundreds of small boats made their way up and down the water, loading and off-loading more sacks and more barrels.

This was Harriet's favourite place in London. The street was called Thames Street because it was right on the river.

Harriet would often take Ginger and meet Nelly at the end of a day. They would walk down here and find somewhere to sit. Then they would stare out at the river and try to imagine the faraway places where so many of the sacks and barrels came from.

Harriet sighed. This time the only thing that was missing was Ginger.

"Mistress Harriet!" cried a voice below them.

Nelly and Harriet looked down on the water.

A young man in a wooden boat looked up at them. The boat was high at the front with a big red T painted on either side.

Harriet blushed. The young man's name was John Taswell.

The three of them had met earlier in the summer. And John seemed to have taken a liking to her.

John's father owned a couple of boats which he and his son rowed up and down the river, carrying goods from the port of London to the warehouses behind them.

"What are two pretty lasses doing by the docks, this afternoon," asked John in a teasing voice.

"And why should John Taswell want to know," said Nelly winking at Harriet.

"Because he would take you for a trip on the river," replied John, propelling his boat towards the shore. "T'is fine boating weather."

Harriet looked at Nelly. "T'would be a good way to Whitehall with our errands," she said, hesitantly. "And t'would be grand to see the city from the water."

Nelly thought for a moment. They had agreed to visit her mother's sister on the other side of the river for the night. She had just had another baby and her mother had made the baby a lace bonnet. If they went with John, they would reach Whitehall faster.

"That would give us more time with Aunt Gwen and the baby," said Nelly. "We would be there well before sunset."

Harriet's heart fluttered in her chest. Nelly's Aunt Gwen was only a few years older than they were. Which meant she was much less strict than other adults. Perhaps she would allow John to take supper with them in her house. And if Nelly was willing...

John Taswell raised his eyebrows. "T'will be past supper before your mind is made up, Mistress Harriet," he said in a low voice.

Harriet made up her mind. "We accept your offer, Master Taswell," she said, blushing again.

Nelly stepped in first.

Harriet followed after, balancing her basket of biscuits with one hand and taking hold of Tom's arm with the other.

A moment later they were out on the river, staring up at the distant spire of St. Paul's Cathedral which looked like a great needle against the clear blue September sky.

Harriet let her eyes wander over the
wooden houses leaning this way and that
into the narrow streets and down to the
river's edge.

Everything seemed so hot and crowded
in the streets. Here on the water there was
a breeze and for the first time the smell of
the city seemed far away.

She thought of poor Ginger running round and round inside his wooden wheel. He would have enjoyed a trip in a boat. Never mind, she would be sure to take him out tomorrow.

3

London's Burning!

It happened in the middle of the night.
The two girls were asleep in the attic
bedroom at Aunt Gwen's house.

Harriet would never forget the sound.
She had been in a deep sleep dreaming
about the King. In her dream, just as in

Nelly's little joke, the King had offered her land and titles in return for the basket of knot biscuits. Even though, in truth, Harriet had left the biscuits with a footman called Christopher who knew her father.

Nevertheless, in her dream, Harriet could feel the thin silk of her grand lady's stockings. She could hear the loud rustle of her grand lady's full silk skirt. Then the dream went peculiar. The skirt and stockings disappeared but the rustle grew louder and louder.

Harriet sat up in bed. Beside her Nelly was still sound asleep.

Harriet ran across the room and looked out the window. The sky was lit up with a dull orange glow. As she watched, the rustling noise turned into a roar and a man came running down the street.

She lifted the catch on the window and pushed it open.

The man's face was black and grimy.
His coat hung in tatters off his back.

"London's burning!" he screamed.
"Citizens awake! Help your neighbours!
London's burning!"

For a moment Harriet couldn't move.
All she could do was stare at the beautiful
orange glow lighting up the sky.

Voices rose from the crowd that had

gathered around the grimy-faced man.

"I'd wager it's them Dutch that started it," cried a thin bearded fellow.

"It was never a Dutchman!" screamed a woman with a young child slung over her hip. "T'was a Catholic spy! The city's full of them!"

The grimy-faced man held up his hand for silence. "T'was a fire in a baker's house in Pudding Lane," he said.

Harriet suddenly froze. There was only one baker in Pudding Lane - and that was her father!

Pictures floated in front of her eyes.

Walter's face was the first. It was his job to light the oven in the middle of night so it would be hot for dawn baking. Twice last week, her father had cuffed him for being drunk and not shutting the oven door properly!

Then she saw her father. He was angry and astonished. But somehow she wasn't worried about her father. He always acted quickly and made the right decisions.

It was the last picture that she dreaded most. It was Ginger. He was barking. He was trapped in his wooden wheel because no-one had remembered to let him out.

"Wake up, Nelly! Wake up!" screamed Harriet, as she pulled on her green dress. "London's on fire!"

Nelly jumped out of bed and stared at the orange sky. She knew London's streets

better than Harriet. "Pudding Lane must be burning!" she said in a hollow voice.

"It is! It is!" screamed Harriet. "They're saying the fire started in our bakery!" Then a strange howl came out of her mouth. "Oh, Nelly! What if Ginger was trapped in the spit wheel?"

Minutes later the two girls were out on the street elbowing their way through a crowd of frightened, angry people.

Everywhere there were carts piled high with boxes and precious cooking pots.

Smoke from burning wooden houses and thatch roofs was being blown across the river. It was black and greasy and choking. The fire couldn't have come at a worse time. Summer had been particularly hot and there had been no rain for weeks.

"We have to cross the river," shouted Nelly in a fierce voice. It was the only way she could keep her courage up. "The bridge is over there! Down that alley!"

They tied themselves together so they couldn't be separated. Then they dodged down the alley.

It was an alley Nelly knew well. It was called Nightingale Lane because a nightingale sang there when the summer nights were still.

As they charged over the muddy ground, Nelly wondered whether there would ever be a still night again.

From round the corner, a man appeared pushing a barrow piled with sacks. Two round-eyed children clung to him like terrified monkeys. "You ain't going over that bridge," shouted the man.

Behind him a woman held a wooden clock in one arm and a crying baby in the other. "The bridge is on fire, see," sobbed the woman. "Everything's on fire."

"What about boats?" shouted Harriet.

"There must be boats on the river."

"Everyone's wanting one," shouted the man. "That's how we came across." He looked at the two girls as if he had suddenly realized how young they were. "It's too dangerous for you, lasses. You best make your way back where you came."

His wife jerked her head towards the river. "There's nought left on the other side," she muttered.

41

"We have to go back," cried Harriet. "We'll take our chances by the river."

The man pointed to a black greasy post sticking up on the shoreline. "That's John Taswell's post," he said. "He's an honest man. If you're quick you'll catch him."

Harriet could have kissed this man she would never see again but Nelly was already dragging her down to the river, shouting John's name at the top of her voice.

4

The River's Burning!

Nothing could have prepared Harriet and
Nelly for the sight that met their eyes
down by the river.

Hundreds of boats bobbed about in
the black greasy water overloaded with
people and their belongings. Men and

women were screaming. Children were crying. Whole families crowded underneath London Bridge, clinging like sodden rats to the stone steps.

On the other side, London looked like one big bonfire. Vast plumes of smoke rose up into the sky. It was impossible to say whether it was morning or evening.

"We can't just stand here gawping," cried Nelly as they looked desperately left and right. "I can't see John's boat anywhere!"

"We'll try further up," shouted Harriet.

Suddenly there was a huge explosion as one of the warehouses on the other side blew up. A shower of sparks shot into the air and spattered down on the water.

For a moment it looked like the river was burning, too!

It must have been the extra light from

the exploding warehouse. Harriet caught sight of a gleaming red T on the front of a greasy boat. It was barely a few metres in front of them.

"There!" she shouted at the top of her voice. "There he is! Hurry!"

Gasping for breath, they slipped and slithered, knee deep in mud, shouting John's name as they went.

John looked up and saw them waving their hands in the air. This time, there were no jolly greetings and laughing questions. He grabbed an oar and immediately pushed the boat through the stinking water

towards the bank.

"Jump!" he shouted. "Jump before someone else does!"

Harriet and Nelly hitched up their skirts, ran the last few metres and because they were tied together they jumped into the front of the boat at the same time.

The greasy wooden boat plunged head first into the river.

Down, down, down it went. Harriet could feel the water pouring over the sides. Neither she nor Nelly could swim and Harriet knew her green woollen dress would drag her straight down to the bottom if she fell in.

Suddenly the boat righted itself!

In her mind's eye, Harriet saw the red T and the wooden sides that seemed so strangely high when she had looked at the boat the day before. Now she understood why. The high sides saved people's lives.

"Cor," cried John. "What a pair of elephants! Pretty you may be, but clumsy you *certainly* are!" He laughed and began to row. "Never seen anything like it!"

Harriet and Nelly looked at each other. They were two gasping crumpled heaps on either side of a greasy wooden boat. Their clothes were torn. Their faces were black and shiny with sweat.

But it was good to hear the sound of someone laughing. Somehow it gave Harriet hope that Ginger was still alive.

5

Lost and Found

As the boat touched the other side, Harriet and Nelly scrambled out. They had learnt their lesson. This time they went separately.

"I'm coming, too," yelled John.

"No!" shouted Harriet. "Wait for us on the water."

Then to John's total astonishment, she leant over and kissed him on the cheek. The two girls turned and pushed through the tide of people pouring out of the city.

Lines of men were passing buckets of water from the river to the blaze. Soldiers, ankle deep in stinking mud, pulled down bunches of burning thatch with long metal hooks to stop the fire spreading from roof to roof.

But nothing made any difference.
A strong wind was blowing.
It picked up handfuls of flaming
straw and tossed them every
which way.

Suddenly a woman ran
screaming down the street.
Her dress was on fire
but she wouldn't drop the
bundle she was carrying.
She banged straight into
Harriet and Nelly.

In the confusion that followed, Harriet lost sight of Nelly.

But Harriet had no time to look for her. She had to find Ginger!

Desperately searching for a familiar landmark, Harriet ran down the nearest street. Ahead of her a carved lion swung crazily from the front of a burning house.

Her heart leapt in her chest. The burning house was the Red Lion Tavern! She was only a street away from Pudding Lane!

Sobbing for breath, she raced past the tavern and turned down the end of Pudding Lane.

Blackened timbers leaned drunkenly against each other. Everything was covered in soot and ash.

Harriet's head began to spin.

The picture she had dreaded most was

in front of her.

Pudding Lane was gone and Ginger was gone with it.

Harriet felt herself falling.

Then everything went black.

53

Four days later, Harriet opened her eyes. She was back in the attic bedroom at Aunt Gwen's house on the other side of the river.

Voices floated around the room. They seemed to be coming from somewhere near the ceiling.

"She's going to be fine," said one voice. Harriet knew that one. It was Nelly's mother.

"Thank goodness," cried her father's voice. "I just can't understand why she went home when she was safe here."

Harriet was puzzled. Why was her father being so stupid? Of course he knew why she went home.

It was for Ginger.

Tears filled her eyes and all she could hear was a roaring that seemed to get louder and louder.

"Bring him to her," cried Nelly's voice. "It'll make her better! I know it will!"

"I'll fetch him!" said John Taswell's voice.

A moment later, something rough and stinky was pushed in front of Harriet's face. It smelt of pork fat and soot.

She lifted an arm to push the thing away. But it came back. This time it shoved a wet nose in her face.

Then it barked.

The roaring in Harriet's head stopped. She opened her eyes.

Two little brown eyes with hairy lashes stared into hers.

"It's Ginger, lass," said her father's voice. "It's Ginger. He was tied to my belt when I found you. Don't you remember?"

As Harriet looked up at her father's dark worried face, slowly, she began to remember. He had caught her as she fell at the end of Pudding Lane. He had carried her back to the river. John had taken them all across, herself, her father, Nelly and her mother, and Ginger.

Tears welled up in her eyes and made them sting. How could she have forgotten?

"Ginger!" whispered Harriet but the tears kept pouring down her face.

"Harriet!" cried Nelly. "Why are you crying? Ginger is safe."

Harriet sniffed and tried to wipe away her tears. "Promise you won't be angry with me, father," she whispered.

"Promise."

Harriet hugged the smelly little terrier who meant so much to her. "My new dress," she began. "It's ruined."

Then something extraordinary happened.

Her father held up a green woollen dress.
It was just like the one she had been given.

And there wasn't a mark on it!

For a moment Harriet looked totally
bewildered.

"Ma made you a new one, silly!" cried Nelly. "So you see, there's nothing to worry about. Everyone is safe. The fire is over."

Harriet looked at the ring of faces smiling down at her. Then she looked at Ginger. He was already asleep in the crook of her arm.

Nelly was right. There was nothing to worry about at all.

Harriet closed her eyes and fell immediately into a deep dreamless sleep.

Notes

The King's Biscuits

During the time of the Stuarts, there were great changes in baking. Cakes and fancy biscuits appeared for the first time. People began to eat salads and French ways of cooking became more commonplace.

The Great Fire of London

The fire started in Thomas Farynor's bakery in Pudding Lane in the early morning of September 2, 1666. It lasted for five days and burned down more than 13,000 houses. Records of the time say no more than half a dozen people died. However, the fire killed millions of rats, so the spread of plague was finally halted.